Vincent, Gabrielle.
[Jour, un chien. English]
A day, a dog / Gabrielle Vincent —1st American ed.
p. cm.
Summary: Pictures tell the story of a dog's day, from the moment he is abandoned on the highway until he finds a friend in a young boy.
ISBN 1-886901-51-0 (alk. paper)
[1. Dogs--Fiction. 2. Stories without words.] I. Title.

PZ7.V744 Day 2000
[E]--dc21
99-047297

Originally published under the title *un jour, un chien*
by Éditions DUCULOT

Printed in Spain

Third printing

Gabrielle Vincent

a day, a dog

FRONT STREET
Asheville, North Carolina
2000

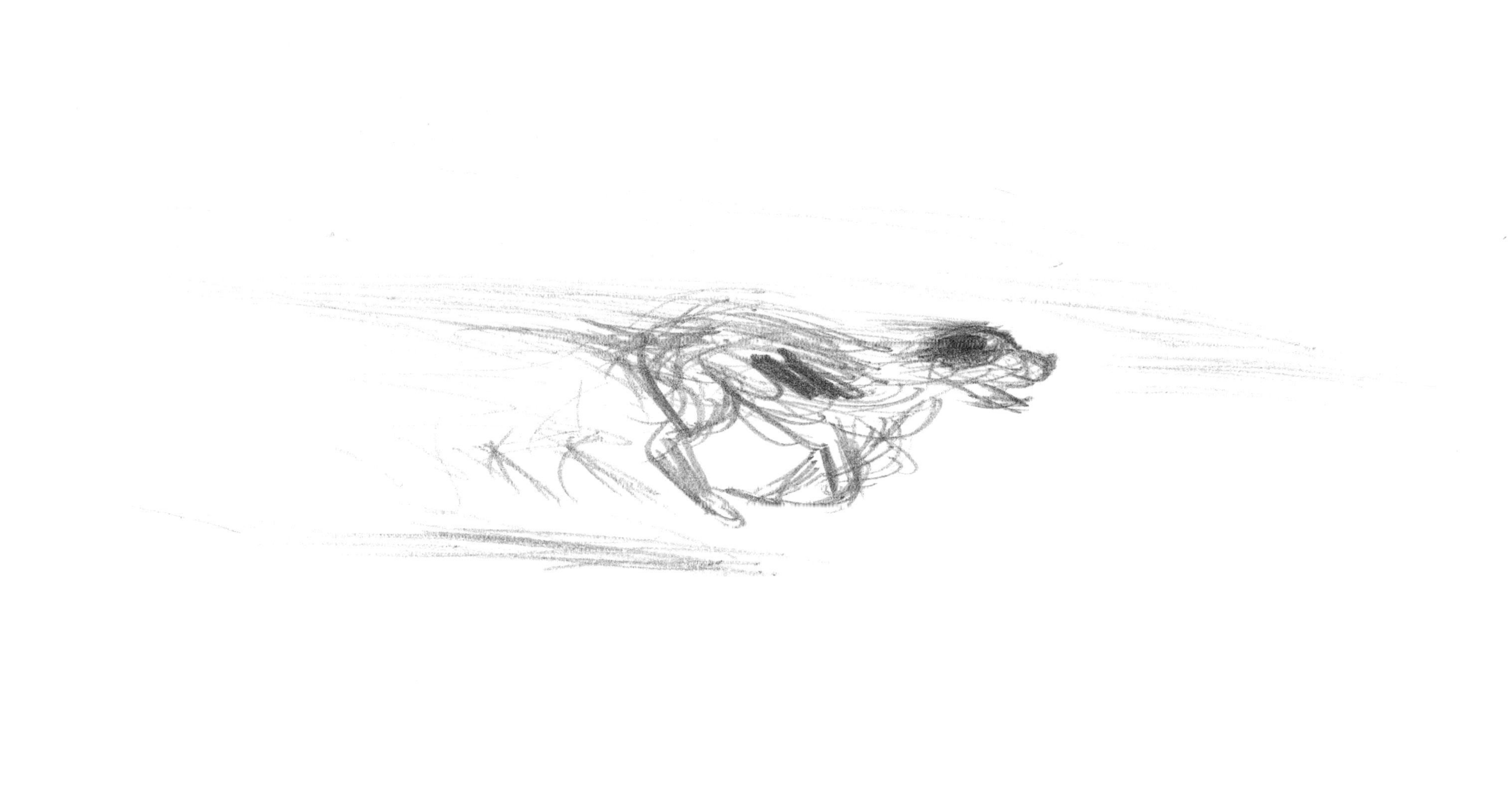

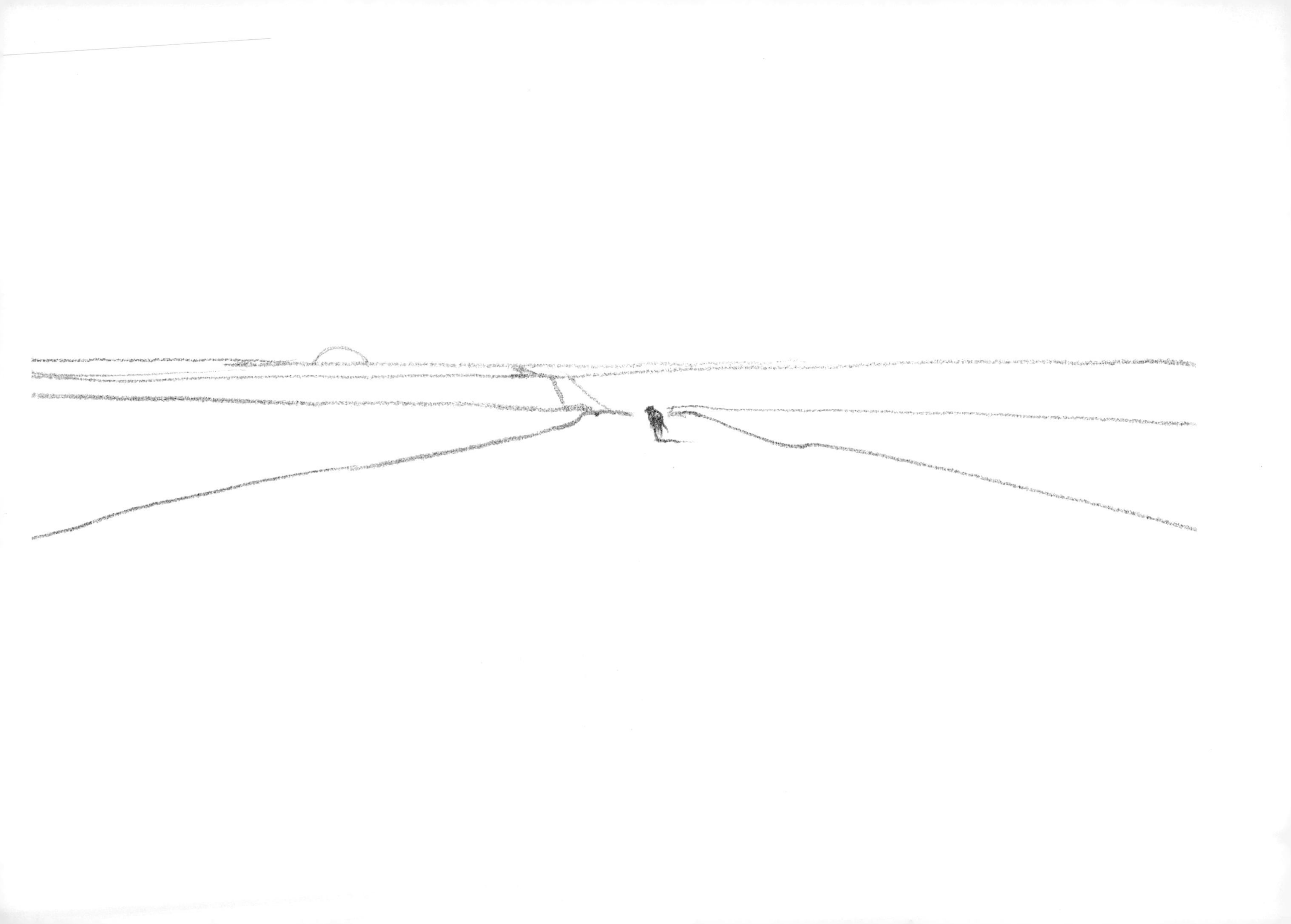

VERMONT STATE COLLEGES
0 00 03 0685263 3